Hide and
Go Fetch

Get your paws on all of the Puppy Powers books!

#1: A Wishbone Come True

#2: Wag, You're It!

#3: Take a Bow-Wow

Puppy Powers

Hide and Go Fetch

BY KRISTIN EARHART
ILLUSTRATED BY VIVIENNE TO

Scholastic Inc.

5546 7889
12/14

ISBN 978-0-545-61762-8

Text copyright © 2014 by Kristin Earhart
Cover and interior art copyright © 2014 by Scholastic Inc.

12 11 10 9 8 7 6 5 4 3 2 1   14 15 16 17 18 19/0
Printed in the U.S.A.   40
First printing, November 2014

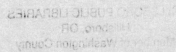

To Rusty Ulman, who has a wonderful, well-trained family

⭐ Chapter 1 ⭐

"No fair. You went first yesterday," Henry McCoy said, rushing toward the bathroom door.

"And I'm going first today," Abby responded. Abby was two years older and barely two inches taller, but she still managed to glare down at Henry.

"You'll take *forever*. You'll brush your teeth and brush your hair and put on bubble-gum lip gloss." Henry counted the tasks on his hands, just to annoy his sister.

"I'm faster, so I should get to go first." He tried to push past her.

"You aren't faster, because I'm already in." She slid through the open crack and slammed the door behind her. She just missed getting her blond ponytail caught in the doorjamb.

Would've served her right, Henry thought. He gave the door an angry shove. "No fair."

"I'll tell you what isn't fair," their mom said, striding out of her bedroom. "Having to listen to you two fight at this hour." Henry looked at his mom. She was all puffy around the eyes, and there was a pillow-crease across her face. "I haven't even had coffee yet."

"But she's just in there wasting a lot of time," Henry complained. "She's probably practicing blowing kisses at Simon Jay in the mirror!"

"I do not like Simon Jay!" Abby protested through the door.

"Well, that's a relief," their dad muttered, shuffling into the hallway. He put an understanding hand on his wife's shoulder as he headed for the stairs. "I'll start the coffee," he promised.

It was a fairly typical morning in the McCoy house. Henry felt bad for his parents. Then he heard the slow *swish, swish, swish* of mouthwash in the bathroom, and he was angry with Abby all over again. "She takes *forever*!" he complained.

His mom sighed. "Open the door, Abigail," she said, knocking. "Let's talk this through."

Abby immediately opened the door. She was holding a bright blue brush and some no-frizz hair spray.

"Okay, kids," their mom began. "What seems to be the problem?"

"She never lets me go first," Henry explained. "I only ever need, like, two seconds."

"That's because you never wash your hands after you go to the bathroom," Abby insisted. "It's disgusting."

Mom's eyebrows bunched together. "What's disgusting is that you two can't get along for more than two seconds. You can't agree on anything."

Henry and Abby stared at each other. They had the same pale blond hair and the same bright blue eyes, but that's where the similarities ended. There was, however, one thing they had in common.

"That's not exactly true, Mom," Abby said.

"Yeah," Henry admitted. "I hate to say it, but she's right. We can agree on something." He paused to make sure their mom was listening. "We agree that our family needs a dog."

"For goodness' sake!" Their mom's lips puffed out as she sighed with disbelief. "Wait a second. You're not going to argue with him, Abby?"

Henry's sister shook her head.

"Are you sure? You're not going to disagree, just to bother him?" Their mom seemed annoyed that the kids weren't arguing.

"Nope. I agree," Abby insisted. "A dog is just what this family needs."

Their mom shook her head. "What I need is more sleep. But," she said with a dramatic pause. She held up two fingers. "If you can make it two days without arguing, we can have a serious talk about getting a dog."

"Seriously?" Henry asked.

"Duh," Abby responded. "She said a 'serious' talk."

"Abby, is that how you talk to your brother?" their mom asked. "There will be no dog if you keep acting like that. In fact, I'm adding a day. Now you have to go three days without fighting."

Henry wanted to laugh at his sister. It only took her three seconds to mess up! There was no way she could be nice to him for three whole days. But she had to, and Henry had to help her. For once,

Henry didn't want to get Abby in trouble. For once, they had to work together. He had wanted a dog for too long, and he wasn't going to miss this chance.

"I'm really sorry, Henry," Abby said. "It wasn't a stupid question."

Their mom's eyebrows jumped to the top of her forehead. Henry couldn't believe it either. An apology from Abby? That was a first.

"Thanks," Henry replied.

"Now, that's more like it," Mrs. McCoy said. "You just have to keep that kind, helpful, understanding attitude up for three days. A dog is a lot of work. You would have to share the dog and share taking care of the dog. You need to prove you can work together before there will be a dog to share."

"Absolutely," Henry said.

"We can do it," Abby agreed.

"If you do, we can go to Power's Pets this weekend. As a family."

"Awesome," Henry said. He knew all about Power's Pets. He and some of his friends had been volunteering at the pet center. Three of his friends had already adopted puppies from there, and all the puppies were cute, smart, and super sweet. The store owner, Mr. Power, had a special talent for finding puppies for possible owners. He had a magic touch for making the perfect match.

"Well," their mom said, "you can start now. Abby, please let your brother in the bathroom."

As they crossed in the bathroom doorway, Abby couldn't hide her scowl. Henry couldn't hide his smug smile. It was going to be a long three days, but it would be worth it.

⭐ Chapter 2 ⭐

"Congratulations. Getting along for three days is a big accomplishment for you two," said Mr. McCoy as the family sat down to brunch at their favorite spot. Actually, it was Abby and Mom's favorite breakfast place. Dad and Henry preferred to get bagels and eat them in the park. But, in the name of compromise, Henry had agreed to go to the restaurant that morning.

"I didn't think you could do it," their mom admitted, "but I'm glad you did."

It had not been easy for Henry. He had had to ignore Abby when she put that I PICK MY NOSE sticker on his back. But he had given Abby a hard time, too. He had put a Post-it on her backpack — a pink Post-it with the name Simon Jay written on it. Around the name, Henry had drawn a big red heart.

Their mother never said they had to be nice to each other. They just couldn't argue.

If putting up with Abby was all he had to do to get a dog, Henry would have learned to get along with her years ago.

"So," their mom said, a fork full of scrambled eggs in her hand, "what kind of dog should we get?"

"It depends what puppies Mr. Power has," Henry explained. "His store works kind of like a shelter. He tries to find homes for puppies who need a family, and he does his best to make a good match — for the people and the dog." He knew all about how the dog adoptions worked.

"Well," Abby began, barely waiting for Henry to finish, "I think we should get a little dog, the kind that sits on your lap."

Henry couldn't stop himself. "That's a terrible idea," he said. "We should get a big dog. They are more laid-back and fun to play with." He ripped a piece off his bagel and shoved it in his mouth. "I'm hoping Mr. Power has a Saint Bernard."

"That's gross," Abby said. "You don't get to vote if you talk with your mouth full. You remind me of a Saint Bernard, too slobbery."

Their mom and dad rolled their eyes. Henry and Abby could be funny when they argued, at least when they weren't all-out annoying.

"Well, for what it's worth," their dad said, "I don't like little, yippy dogs. They bark all the time, just to remind you not to step on them." Henry raised his eyebrows and gave Abby an I-told-you-so look. "But, we also do not have room for a gigantic dog like a Saint Bernard, or its gallons of drool." Abby gave Henry an I-told-you-so look right back.

Their mom just shook her head. "Listen to yourself," she said to her husband. "You wonder why they struggle to find common ground."

"I'm not finished," Mr. McCoy continued, smiling at his wife. "If you kids want a dog, you will both have to compromise. It will be your one final test."

Henry's and Abby's eyes both grew wide with the size of that task. How would they ever be able to choose a puppy together?

Henry had not really thought about how they would choose the puppy. He had thought that they would go into Power's Pets, and he would immediately see the puppy he wanted. He thought he'd instantly know which puppy was perfect for him. When he had thought about this special moment, he hadn't pictured his sister being a part of it.

"I think that's a great plan," Mrs. McCoy said. "You two have been getting along so well this week."

Henry looked at Abby. Of course, they had not told their mom about the pranks they had played on each other that week.

They had not exactly "gotten along." They had just managed to avoid a fight.

"Come on, you two," their dad said. "Don't look so glum. We're about to get a puppy."

"Let's change the subject," Mrs. McCoy said. "Are either of you going to enter the science fair?"

"Probably," Henry said. "If I think of a good topic."

"Of course," Abby said, flashing a boastful smile her brother's way. "I already have a topic, and it can't be beat."

Ugh! Abby had such an attitude! If he could, Henry would share a puppy with anyone other than her.

The McCoys were all in a good mood as soon as they walked into Power's Pets. There was something special about the store. Cheeps, squeaks, and squawks filled the air. The small furry animals ran in their jungle-gym-filled cages. Tropical fish swam around sea grass and coral in huge aquariums. Lucky, Mr. Power's clever black cat, was cuddled up to Chance. Chance was a loveable mutt who acted as the store's own watch dog.

"This place is awesome," said Abby. For once, Henry agreed. He had been having a lot of fun volunteering there with his friends Lexi, Sadie, and Max.

"The puppies are over here." He directed his family to the giant playpen. "Wow, there are a lot today." Henry didn't know if that was a good thing or a bad thing. Would more puppies make it easier to agree with his sister, or nearly impossible?

"They're too cute!" Abby squealed.

"Yes, they are," their mom agreed. She knelt down and put her hand up to the pen. Two fluffy white puppies that looked like tried-and-true lapdogs rushed up to lick her fingers.

Henry spotted a larger pup toward the back. He had black-and-caramel-colored fur with a splash of white from his face down to his chest. "Is that a Bernese mountain dog?" his dad asked.

Henry nodded. "They grow pretty huge," he admitted. The puppy was so fluffy and cuddly, he looked like a stuffed animal. But Dad had said no big dogs.

That's when he saw the Dalmatian. The puppy was mostly white with small black spots on his ears and his body. He was

adorable jogging around the pen, playing with other puppies. He looked over at
Henry with a mischievous expression. The
puppy looked like he had a good sense of
humor. He was a real McCoy!

Henry sighed. The sleek, energetic
Dalmatian was nothing like a lapdog.
There were a lot of dogs that were closer
to Abby's idea of the perfect puppy.

"Hello!" a voice called from the other
side of the pet store. "Henry, is this your

family?" Mr. Power came striding over to the McCoys, his hand stretched out to greet the parents. "It's great to meet you. Henry's been a real help. I'm excited to match you all with a fabulous puppy. It's one way I can show my thanks."

Mr. Power gave Henry his usual kind, knowing smile. "Do you want to meet some of the puppies?"

The McCoys all nodded.

"Maybe you could start by telling me which ones you like," Mr. Power suggested.

Everyone smiled, but no one said anything.

"Cat got your tongue?" Mr. Power asked, laughing. "Just a little pet-store humor," he added. Mr. Power reached into one of the many pockets in his vest. He pulled out four perfect squares of paper. Next, he pulled out four black pens. "Why don't you all write down your three favorite puppies, in order? Then we'll look at the lists and try to compromise."

Mr. Power handed each McCoy a slip of paper and a pen. "I'm sure you'll all be able to come to an agreement, right?" When he smiled at Henry, he had a twinkle in his eye.

Henry had always thought there was something special about Power's Pets, but it would take some real magic to make all four McCoys agree on anything.

Chapter 3

Of course, Henry was going to put the Dalmatian first. How could he not? That puppy looked so clever and fun. He was full of personality with his playful expression, floppy ears, and curled tail.

He had a feeling his mom and sister would choose one of the superfluffy dogs. There were lots of cute ones. His dad, on the other hand, liked sporting dogs like retrievers.

He felt bad for Mr. Power. How would that nice old man deal with his stubborn family?

Henry decided to list the Bernese mountain dog second. He put a black Lab third, in case it was one of his dad's favorites. Then he handed his slip to Mr. Power. He crossed his fingers and watched as his sister, mom, and dad gave their papers to the store owner as well.

Mr. Power shuffled through the sheets, mumbling to himself. "I can tell the McCoys all have very strong opinions."

"We try to teach the kids that it's important to know what you want," Mrs. McCoy said.

"Yes," Mr. Power replied. "I believe that's a good lesson. Right up there with learning how to get along and work well with others."

Uh-oh. Both Henry and Abby slumped a little. Did Mr. Power know about their history?

"But that seems to come easily for your family," Mr. Power said. "Without even knowing it, you all compromised wonderfully."

The McCoys looked around at one another, confused.

"Every one of you put the Dalmatian first on your list," the store owner declared. "You all seem to like him. Let's hope he likes you." Mr. Power reached into the puppy pen and lifted up the spotted pup.

Henry couldn't believe it. They all wanted the Dalmatian! But the puppy had to want them, too. That was how things worked at Power's Pets.

As soon as Mr. Power put the puppy on the ground, he began to run circles around the McCoys. The Dalmatian looked up at Mr. McCoy and barked happily. He jumped on Mrs. McCoy's legs and panted. He ran a figure eight around Abby's legs and then galloped over to Henry. Henry got on his knees to pet the hyper puppy. Just as Henry reached out, the pup ran behind him. Henry laughed and waited, but the little spotted puppy didn't race out the other side.

"Where'd he go?" Henry asked. The room was silent. He looked over his shoulder but didn't see anything.

Just then, the rest of the family burst out laughing. Henry looked down and saw the puppy peeking out from behind him. The puppy quickly pulled his head back, and then looked out again with the most mischievous grin.

"He's playing peekaboo," Mrs. McCoy said.

"Boo," said Henry. The puppy trotted around and put his paws on Henry's knees. "Boo," Henry repeated, and the puppy barked. He wagged his tail.

"Boo!" Abby called. The young dog wheeled around and bounded to her. "He thinks it's his name," Abby said.

"Maybe Boo *is* his name," suggested Mr. Power.

Surprisingly, it was that easy. The McCoy family had agreed on something else: Their new puppy's name was Boo.

"It's unanimous," Mr. McCoy said.

"What does that mean?" asked Henry.

"It means absolutely everyone agrees," his dad explained. "Like a unanimous decision."

"I'm happy you all like Boo," Mr. Power said with a clap of his hands. "It's great to match another one of my volunteers with such a special puppy."

Henry smiled. It was hard to believe. Lexi, Max, and Sadie had all adopted puppies. Now it was finally his turn. He was going to have an adorable puppy of his very own. Well, not exactly. He would have an adorable puppy that he'd have to share with his annoying sister.

While their parents filled out paperwork, Mr. Power told Abby and Henry about Boo's special talent.

"It's a really cool trick," the store owner said. "But please take care. Whenever you do tricks with young dogs, you should be extremely patient and kind. Dogs respond to their owners' emotions. They are very smart that way." He gave Boo a few long pets, but the pup tried to squirm out of his arms. "You know, Boo is pretty excited now, so I won't ask him to do the trick. But I'll tell you how to." Mr. Power went on to explain the trick, step-by-step. It was cool. Boo could catch a ball in midair. Henry couldn't wait to see that.

Before they left, the McCoys bought a red collar (Henry's favorite color) and a blue leash (Abby's favorite color). They had compromised. Somehow, Boo made it easier to get along with Abby. The puppy had enough energy and cuteness for everyone.

The first weekend with their puppy was super fun. It was hard for Henry and Abby to go to school on Monday. At recess, Henry finally got to talk to his friend Max. Max also volunteered at Power's Pets. He had an adorable golden retriever named Bear.

"I can't wait for Bear to meet Boo at the dog park," Henry said.

"Yeah," Max agreed. "I remember when Bear was a tiny guy."

Henry remembered that, too. He couldn't believe how quickly all of his friends' puppies had gotten big. He had a hard time picturing Boo as a full-grown dog.

"Hey, does Boo have a special trick?" Max asked.

Henry whacked himself on the fore-head. "I totally forgot," Henry exclaimed.

"What does he do?" Max prodded.

"I haven't seen it yet," Henry explained. "Mr. Power said he can catch a ball in midair."

"That sounds cool," Max said. "You've got to get him to do it. Seriously."

Henry looked at his friend. Why was Max so serious about his puppy's trick? He would have to wait to see.

☆ Chapter 4 ☆

When Henry got home from school, Boo was waiting for him at the door. "Hey, boy," Henry greeted his new puppy. "Come on!" Henry raced up to his room with Boo close behind. Henry had one thing on his mind: the trick. He quickly crawled under his bed to get his red handball. Boo trotted under the bed from the other side. The puppy toddled up to Henry and licked his face.

"Yes, Boo," Henry said, his words

squeezed between giggles. "I missed you today, too."

Henry scooted out and tossed the ball in the air. "Let's try your trick, Boo."

The puppy began to yip and run in circles. Henry tried to remember what Mr. Power had said. The store owner had made a big deal about staying calm. He had told Henry and Abby to give the puppy their full attention. It was an important part of doing tricks.

"That's a good boy," Henry said in a soft, soothing voice. Next he thought of the cue — the words that told Boo it was time to do his trick. "Boo, do you see the ball?" he began. "Let me see you fetch!" Those were the words. Boo lifted his ears and cocked his head to one side. Next, Henry tossed the ball nice and high. Boo launched himself into the air, leaping to clench the ball between his teeth. When he landed, Boo was clearly proud of himself. Henry was proud, too. He reached out to congratulate his puppy and took the slobbery ball from his mouth.

"You're such a good boy, Boo!" he exclaimed. The puppy scampered around in excitement. Red and blue sparkles began to whiz through the air, in circles around Boo.

"What's that?" Henry murmured, watching the sparkles. Wondering if he was seeing things, Henry looked in the mirror. Just as he had guessed, he couldn't see any sparkles there. Was he imagining things? He glanced back at the mirror. He saw Boo. He saw his desk. He saw his bed. And he saw the ball floating in the air. Wait, what? Henry looked down at the ball in his hand, except he couldn't see his hand. He looked in the mirror again. He wasn't there — he was invisible!

The puppy yipped with glee. "Boo?" Henry asked. "Did you do this? Is this your trick?" Boo yipped again. "This is so cool!" Henry did a crazy celebration dance. He looked in the mirror. He still couldn't see anything but Boo's red ball bouncing around in midair!

Henry started panting with excitement. "What should I do? How long does it last? What should I do?" Boo could not answer these questions.

"I'll bug Abby!" he announced with a

shiver of mischief. He headed for the door. Boo pranced behind him. "You have to be quiet," he whispered to the energetic puppy. But Boo was more excited than ever.

When Henry arrived at Abby's room, he discovered the door was locked. "Downstairs," he mouthed to Boo, before realizing the pup couldn't see him or his mouth. Somehow, though, Boo seemed to be able to bounce all around Henry's legs without running into him. Unfortunately, Henry did not have the same luck. He couldn't tell where his own feet were. He tripped over the rug in the hallway. Then, when he reached out for the railing on the stairs, he missed. His body fell forward. The carpet on the steps burned his cheek as he slid down the stairs headfirst. The next thing he knew, he was flat on the wood floor at the bottom of the staircase.

Henry blinked and sat up. Boo was there, licking his knee. It pounded with heat.

"What was that?" Henry's mom rushed in from the garage. "Abby? Henry?" she called. Henry curled himself against the wall as his mom came into the front hall to investigate. "Boo, was that you?" she asked. She glanced up the stairs. "How on earth does such a small dog make such a huge racket?" She patted Boo's head.

"Abby, I'm going back to the garage to tackle the ants!"

"Okay, Mom." Abby's response came from the family room. Henry knew this was his chance to play a prank on his sister. His mom would be in the garage for a long time. The McCoys had a huge ant problem, and Mom would be busy figuring out how they were getting in.

Henry tiptoed to the family room. Abby was there, working on her art project for school. She had pastels spread out in front of her. Henry went closer and saw she was drawing the ocean.

Boo trotted over to Abby for a pet. As his sister leaned over to welcome the puppy, Henry snatched two blue pastels from the table. He slid them under the couch next to her. That seemed like a good trick. She'd have to stop everything to look for them, but she wouldn't suspect Henry had moved them. She'd just assume they had rolled off the side of the table.

A sneaky smile stretched across Henry's face. Then, at the last second, he grabbed a canary yellow pastel and snuck into the kitchen. As he crept away, he realized that the yellow pastel wasn't invisible. It looked like it was floating in midair. He sped up, making sure to hold the bright yellow art supply out of Abby's view.

"Boo, where are you going?" Henry heard Abby say as the puppy ran into the kitchen to find him.

Henry bent down and gave Boo a hug. "Awesome prank, bud," he whispered. "She'll have no clue." His heart raced with excitement. He pictured her searching all around for the missing colors. He loved a simple but effective prank. His mind raced with the possibilities. What else could he do?

That's when he felt his stomach growl. Even invisible stomachs get hungry! Henry walked over to the kitchen counter. He glanced to where Abby was sitting in the other room. She could see into the kitchen, but she was concentrating on her art.

Very carefully, Henry lifted the lid off the muffin tin. Putting down the yellow pastel, he grabbed two muffins with one hand and replaced the lid with the other. *Ping!*

Henry held his breath, hoping Abby didn't hear the clang of the lid. She groaned. Henry quickly hid the muffins under the counter. He couldn't let his sister see floating muffins! When he took a peek, he realized she was searching for her missing art supplies. He smirked.

Henry felt his hands tingle. He looked down and saw the peachy color start to return to his skin. His red sweatshirt was filling in with a pale pink. Henry clutched the muffins to his chest and tiptoed to the hallway and all the way up the stairs. Boo was at his heels. Safe inside his room, he slid down the back side of his door. From there, he could see a faint version of himself in the mirror. He watched with satisfaction as he ate one of his dad's fabulous banana-chocolate-chip muffins. By the time he was done with the second, he was totally visible again.

Chapter 5

"You're not hungry?" Henry's mom asked, looking at her son with concern.

"Not really," Henry answered. The curry dinner smelled good, but Henry didn't have any room.

"It's because he snuck extra muffins after school," Abby said. It was the next day, and Henry had gone back for more muffins. He couldn't say no to those muffins — or the chance to turn invisible again!

His eyes darted over to his sister. "Did you see me take extra muffins?" he asked.

She shrugged. "No, I just had a feeling."

"Let's not place blame," Mr. McCoy said. "But it does seem like this batch of muffins isn't lasting very long."

"And, oddly enough, I found your yellow pastel next to the muffin tin yesterday." Mrs. McCoy smiled at her daughter.

"I was looking for that!" Abby declared. "But it's weird that it was there. I haven't had any muffins since the weekend." Abby glanced over at Henry, who quickly tried to hide his grin.

"I put it in your art kit," their mom said.

Henry was anxious to change the subject. He wasn't going to lie about being invisible. He didn't want to lie at all. If he told them that he had been invisible, would anyone even believe him?

"I thought of an awesome science fair project," Henry said. "It has to do with ants. I want to find out if there are any easy ways to keep ants out of our garage. But I don't want to use poison or sprays since they'd be bad for Boo."

"That would be amazing," his mom said. "Nothing I've tried works. Those ants are everywhere."

"How's your project coming, Abby?" their dad asked.

"Awesome," Abby said. "It is going to be amazing. Just the best." She didn't say anything more.

★　　★　　★

After school the next day, Henry met his friends at the local dog park. It was so cool to see all the puppies together: Luna, Bear, Truffle, and Boo. They romped around and wrestled, yipping joyously. They were all adorable, loyal, and fun.

"It's cool that we all got to adopt puppies from Power's Pets," Max said.

"Yeah," Lexi agreed. She paused and glanced around the group. The friends were different in lots of ways, but their love of dogs was something they all had in common. "Having a new puppy can be pretty magical." Lexi's eyebrows were raised, hinting at a hidden meaning.

Max and Sadie nodded. Henry did, too. They all looked thoughtful.

"I think the best part is how well Truffle seems to know me," Sadie said, watching her cream puff of a pup. "He's taught me a lot about myself."

Henry smiled to himself. Sadie was always so serious! Henry didn't feel like Boo had all that much to teach him. He was just excited to have an adorable puppy who could do a special trick — a trick that made him invisible. All Henry wanted was to figure out how to make the most of it. He loved his puppy, and he was certain his new super ability was going to be nothing but fun.

"Is anyone doing the science fair?" Lexi asked.

"I'm thinking about it," Max said.

"Probably not. It's the same day as this thing I have for piano," Sadie said.

"I have to," Henry answered.

"No you don't. It's optional," Lexi insisted. "No one *has* to do it."

"I do," said Henry. "Abby is doing it, and she thinks her idea is *the* best, so I have to try to beat her."

"Well, okay," Lexi said, shrugging. "If

you have to beat her, I guess you have to do the science fair."

Henry tried to hide his frown. Sometimes Lexi reminded him of his sister.

He wished he could explain what it was like to live with Abby. She was so sure of herself, always claiming to be older and wiser. Just once, he wanted to feel like more than her little brother.

Henry looked around his circle of friends. Lexi had a brother. Max had a brother and sister. But they didn't seem to be as competitive as Henry and Abby. And Sadie was an only child, although she was sometimes competitive with herself. Henry sighed. None of them could understand.

⭐ Chapter 6 ⭐

"Henry, Abby!" Mrs. McCoy called from the bottom of the stairs. "We're ready to go. Bring your lists."

It was the next afternoon, and the whole family was headed into town. Boo was coming, too! He sat in the backseat between Abby and Henry.

"Seat belts," Mr. McCoy said as he started the car and backed it out of the garage.

Henry and Abby needed to get supplies

for their science fair projects. Henry had done some research on the computer. He wanted to buy things that ants didn't like.

"Lemons, cinnamon, and baby powder," his mom read out loud. "Funny. I like all these things," she said.

"But you don't like ants," Henry reminded her.

His mom bobbed her head from side to side as she thought about what he said. "I guess ants and I don't have much in common." She looked at the list again and said that they'd find everything he needed at the grocery store.

"I can get almost all my stuff at the hardware store," Abby said once they were on their way. Abby handed her tightly folded list to their mom in the front seat. "Could you just pick up two big potatoes for me?"

Mrs. McCoy scanned Abby's list. "Sure thing," she answered.

Ugh! *Why didn't Mom read Abby's list out loud?* Henry wondered. He was so curious about his sister's project. *How did potatoes and hardware supplies make a science experiment?*

Henry and Mom hit the grocery store first. Mom actually dug deep into the crate to find a large potato. "I think this is about as big as they come," Mom announced, holding one up.

"It's as big as Abby's head," Henry said.

"That's not true," his mom said. "You don't sound very much like a scientist. Scientists do not exaggerate." She rummaged through the bin again to select another one.

Henry was relieved that his mom could take a joke. "I promise not to exaggerate about the ants," he said.

"You can't exaggerate about them. They are wretched, pesky invaders. The worst!" She shook her fist, holding a very large potato, in the air. Sometimes Henry's mom took a joke too far. They shopped for some stuff for dinner, grabbed more bananas for muffins, and headed to the checkout.

Before they even reached the car, Abby was striding toward the hardware store. "Come on, Dad!" she called from the sidewalk.

As soon as Dad got out of the backseat, Henry scooted in. He scooped up Boo in his arms. Henry kissed the puppy's head and gave him a big scratch all over. He watched his dad and sister disappear into the hardware store. It was only four doors down from the grocery store. He was tempted to go up to the window and peek inside. Maybe he could figure out her plan.

But then Boo swiped his tongue across Henry's face, and Henry decided to stay in the car with his puppy. What could be more fun than that?

The next day after school, Henry gathered all his supplies and headed for the garage. Ants were making trails everywhere. "I've got a lot of work to do," he told Boo as the puppy snuffled around the garage.

Boo liked to smell everything: the base-ball equipment, the oil spot on the floor, the tub of clothes for Goodwill. When Boo and his nose got to one of the ant trails, the puppy stopped. He gave the ants a strong sniff and sneezed. *Woof!* Boo barked. He ran circles around the ants and barked again. *Woof, woof!*

Henry tried to ignore his puppy. He wanted his project to be as scientific as possible. He was going to try to create a barrier that would keep the ants from crossing into the garage. First, he drew a straight line across the garage with chalk. Next, he measured the line. He divided it into three parts. There was a part for each

substance he was testing as an ant barrier: baby powder, cinnamon, and lemon juice.

"Boo, stop distracting me," Henry said as he tried to mark the line. The puppy thought the measuring tape was a toy. He had already knocked over the jar of cinnamon twice and put his paw in the bowl of lemon juice. But the worst part was that the puppy kept walking right over Henry's line. Boo was hunting down the ants. He was following them everywhere, even when it meant stepping on the barrier line.

"All right, that's it, buddy," Henry finally declared when the puppy started to examine the container of baby powder. Henry remembered that puppies shouldn't breathe in stuff like that. The fine powder could be bad for their lungs. "Let's put you inside."

After Boo was out of the way, Henry really got to work. For the first section, he

★ 53 ★

used the baby powder. He cleaned up the part of the line that Boo had messed up. Next, he used the cinnamon. For the third and final section, he dipped a sponge in lemon juice and wiped it along the barrier line.

Satisfied with his good work, Henry cleaned up and went back inside. He found his mom sorting dirty clothes into piles. "Success?" she asked.

"I don't know. We have to wait to see if ants stop coming into the garage," Henry explained.

"How long?"

"A couple of days?" he answered, but he wasn't entirely sure. Chances were, there would still be ants, but Henry hoped he could follow their trails. If the ants did not go over one part of the barrier, he would know they were avoiding that substance. Henry's guess was that they would purposely stay away from the lemon juice.

"For the experiment to work, no one can step on the lines. If anyone tracks the powder or cinnamon, it will mess up the results."

"Uh-huh," his mom murmured as she sprayed stain remover on a white shirt.

"So Boo can't go in the garage," Henry explained. Mom nodded.

"And you and Dad can't park the car in the garage."

"Seriously?" Mom asked, looking up.

"Only for a few days," said Henry. "I just need the barrier to stay intact."

Mom agreed to park in the driveway for a couple of days, in the name of science.

⭐ Chapter 7 ⭐

After talking to his mom, Henry grabbed a snack. He felt kind of bored, so he looked for Boo. No one with a magic puppy should ever feel bored! "Hey, Boo," Henry said when he found the pup in his bedroom. "Let's do something."

Henry already had something in mind. It had nothing to do with banana muffins, for once, but everything to do with Abby's science project. "I'm not really allowed in Abby's room," Henry explained to his puppy. "I'll be in and out and won't touch anything. But we should use your trick, just in case." Abby was at track practice, so Henry thought he'd have plenty of time.

While still in his room, Henry gave Boo several longs pets. He wanted to calm him down. Next, Henry held up a ball. "Boo, do you see the ball?" he asked. "Let me see you fetch." At once, the puppy's ears pricked up. He sat back on his hind legs, ready. Once Henry threw the ball in the air, Boo sprang up and caught it in one smooth motion. Henry soon saw the blue and red stars swirl around. He held his hand out and watched as it started to disappear. In just a few seconds, he was invisible.

"Okay, bud," Henry said. "Let's go." Boo circled Henry, excited.

First, Henry tried Abby's door. As he suspected, it was locked, so he headed to the bathroom. In the medicine cabinet, he found an old bobby pin with a blue butterfly on it. With Boo right on his heels, he went back to Abby's room and started to pick the lock. He'd seen it on TV lots of times. Sure enough, he heard a click and the door popped open. Henry tiptoed in. He felt like a spy.

He didn't have to open drawers or locate a safe. Abby's project was right on her desk. "Whoa," Henry said before he could stop himself. He had to remember: Spies are always silent.

Quiet as can be, Boo jumped on a chair and put his paws on the desk. The puppy admired Abby's hard work.

The two potatoes lay right in the center of the desk. Loops of copper wires, clips, and nails poked out of them. There was also a clock connected to the whole mess, and the numbers said the right time. Henry was amazed. Abby had made some kind of crazy potato clock.

Just then, he heard a door slam. He froze. He looked at the clock. It was too early for Abby to be home, wasn't it? Then he heard footsteps on the stairs. "Come on, Boo," he whispered. "Hurry!" He had just turned to leave when he heard a loud *crunch*. Henry looked back and froze. Boo was sitting on the desk chair with the potato clock dangling from his mouth.

"Boo!" Abby cried from the hallway. "You can't eat that!"

As soon as the puppy saw her, he opened his mouth, and the clock tumbled to the floor.

Henry threw himself against the wall as his sister stormed into the room. He could tell Abby was furious. He knew that look.

Despite her anger, Abby was still very gentle with the startled puppy. "Boo, open your mouth. Give it to me." Abby worked quickly. "That's a good boy," she soothed. "You don't want to eat that. It'll make you really sick." Abby pulled a chunk of potato from the puppy's mouth. A loud buzz came from the clock on the ground, but Abby didn't seem to notice. She was just taking care of Boo.

Henry felt a tingle in his finger, and he noticed a pale pink start to spread up his

hand. He was becoming visible. He had to get out of there!

"How'd you get in here, Boo?" Abby wondered. "Maybe Mom needed something in my room. Let's go check." With that, Abby got up and jogged into the hallway, Boo cradled in her arms.

As soon as the coast was clear, Henry rushed back to his room. He could now see his hands and feet. When he looked in the mirror, he could also see the expression on his face. It was a pale version, but it was him. In the mirror, he didn't look like a kid who had just turned invisible. He didn't look cool and adventurous like a spy. He looked bummed. He had snuck into his sister's room to see her supercool science project, and now it was ruined.

At dinner that night, Henry didn't have much to say. He wanted to apologize to Abby, but he didn't know how.

"The clock broke when it hit the floor," Abby announced. "I'll have to start from scratch, or I might just come up with another science project."

"That's too bad," Mr. McCoy said. "I'm sure we could get all the parts again. This time, we'd have to make sure your bedroom door stays closed — now that we know Boo likes raw potatoes."

"We'll see," Abby replied with a shrug. "I found out Simon Jay's doing a potato clock, too, and I don't want him to think I copied." She drew figure eights with her spoon in her bowl. The fact that Dad had made cream-of-potato soup was just a reminder of the messy events of the afternoon.

"I like your hair like that, honey," their mom said, obviously trying to cheer up Abby.

Abby' lifted her hand to touch the butterfly bobby pin that clipped back her bangs.

"Thanks," she mumbled. "I just found this on my desk." As she said it, her eyes flitted over to Henry. They narrowed.

Henry quickly looked at his soup. There were all kinds of questions stirring around in his head. Did Abby know how the bobby pin got there? Did she know that he had been in her room? And, the biggest question of all, did she know about Boo's invisibility trick?

Henry was pretty sure she didn't. If she did, she'd have told their parents by now. Whether or not Abby knew, Henry felt bad. Yes, they were always playing pranks on each other and being competitive, but they were still brother and sister. He hadn't wanted to ruin her project, especially since it was so cool. He wanted to make it up to her, but how?

⭐ Chapter 8 ⭐

The next afternoon, Henry still hadn't confessed to Abby. He kept thinking about his problem during hip-hop class, and he messed up his dance moves every time. As he walked home, he decided he would just come out and tell her. He didn't have to say anything about being invisible. He just needed to apologize for unlocking her door and letting Boo eat her science project. After all, he never meant to mess it up. But apologizing to Abby was never easy.

Turning the corner to his house, he told

himself he'd talk to Abby first thing. He patted his mom's car as he walked toward the front door. Mom and Dad had both been parking in the driveway ever since Henry had set up his science project.

Henry put his jacket and backpack in the front hall and headed to the family room. Abby wasn't working on her art project at the table, so he went to the kitchen.

"Hey, Dad," he said. Mr. McCoy was shaking some spices into a pot on the stove.

"Hey, bud," his dad said. "How was school?"

"Oh, you know," Henry answered.

"No, I don't," his dad replied. "I wasn't there."

"It was good," Henry said, but he wasn't really thinking about school. He was thinking about his sister. "Do you know where Abby is?" he asked.

Mr. McCoy sighed. "Come to think of it, I haven't seen her in a while. Maybe she's somewhere with Boo. I saw him come racing through here a bit ago. He was running in circles. That is one silly pooch."

Henry left the kitchen and was about to head upstairs when he heard a bark. Henry was sure it was Boo's excited yip. It sounded like he was outside. When Henry looked in the backyard, there was no Boo. Maybe Abby was playing with him in the front. He opened the front door. No Boo. When he heard the bark again, Henry thought it was coming from the garage.

Oh, no. The garage! Henry ran inside and whipped open the door to the garage. The light was on, and there was Boo, running around in tight, giddy circles.

"No, Boo!" Henry cried. There were perfect little paw prints in baby powder and cinnamon everywhere. It was like finger painting for puppies. "Oh, Boo," he murmured. "How'd you get in here?" The puppy ran over to Henry and jumped up, putting his paws on Henry's legs. He smelled like a baby — and cinnamon toast. Henry was worried that Boo had inhaled the powder. He checked his puppy's nose. He was relieved when it looked clean.

Next, he glanced over to where he had created the ant barrier, and he knew that his project was ruined. Boo had run through the baby powder, cinnamon, and lemon juice and tracked it all over. The ants had already found trails through the barrier. Henry couldn't keep those six-legged pests away. "You really want to be part of the science fair, don't you, Boo?" Henry asked. "First you messed up Abby's project, now mine."

Boo squirmed away from Henry and raced over to the parade of ants. He sniffed a cluster here and chased after a row of ants heading there. The puppy seemed as intent on tracking down the ants as Henry's mom.

Henry quickly caught Boo and lifted

him up. He walked closer to the lines he had made. Suddenly, he realized there was something suspicious going on. He saw all kinds of paw prints . . . and the print of a sneaker. When he looked over at the baby powder, he saw another sneaker print, and another. In fact, sneaker prints appeared as he watched. There were prints, but no sneakers. Those were the sneakiest sneakers ever!

"Abby," Henry whispered, "I know you're there."

Henry heard a rush of footsteps. Boo leaped from his arms and ran inside. The puppy had to be right on Abby's tail!

Henry followed his puppy through the hallway and up the stairs. Boo turned the corner to Abby's room and ran straight in. Then the door seemed to slam shut all by itself — right in Henry's face.

Henry knocked on the door. "Abby, let me in." He pressed his nose right up to the door.

"I don't have to," Abby hissed. "Maybe you should go find a bobby pin and break in."

"Abby, I didn't mean to —"

"Yeah, right. You didn't mean to pick the lock on my door?" Abby snarled. "Or you didn't mean to let our puppy eat stuff that's really bad for him?"

"I didn't know Boo was going to eat the potato!" Henry had wanted to apologize, but now Abby had made him mad all over again.

"You're lucky I didn't tell Mom and Dad," Abby said through the door.

"Well, I can tell on you, too," Henry pointed out. "You messed up my science project on purpose. And there are foot-prints on the garage floor to prove it."

At that moment, the door swung back open. Abby looked almost see-through, but her face had a full-on scowl. It was weird, seeing her in between invisible and normal.

"It was not on purpose," Abby declared. "And I didn't mean to let Boo in. He just pushed his way into the garage and started to chase the ants. I tried to get him away, but he wouldn't listen." She huffed. "You know what it's like to make a mistake. Don't you?" Henry thought that his sister's face matched her voice: bratty.

At once, Boo started to whine. He looked from Abby to Henry with his gigantic, sad, cocoa-colored eyes. He whimpered.

"You're upsetting Boo," Henry said. Boo hunched down and put his paws over his ears. "Don't talk like that around my puppy." Henry immediately wanted to take it back. "Our puppy," he corrected himself.

"Is that what this is all about?" Abby asked. "You think he's yours. And you're upset that he does the trick for me, too."

"No, that's not true," Henry insisted.

"I think it is. I'll bet you that he'll do the trick for me before he does it for you," Abby said, kneeling to the floor and picking up a blue ball.

"Oh, no you don't," Henry retorted. In an instant, he was scrambling to his room to get a ball, too. He found the red ball he always used for the trick and ran back. Abby was already holding her blue ball in the air.

Boo was still whining. His eyes were full of concern, but he didn't take them off of the blue ball. One look and Henry knew they shouldn't ask him to do the trick. The puppy was confused.

★ 71 ★

But as soon as Abby began to recite the words, Henry chimed in.

"Boo, can you see the ball?" they both called out. "Let me see you fetch!"

Abby and Henry threw their balls in the air. The blue and red balls made perfect arcs, and Boo tracked them both. At the moment the balls' paths crossed, Boo bolted up. He made a mighty leap and nabbed both the blue and the red ball at the exact same time.

Henry and Abby looked at each other in shock. "Are we both going to turn invisible?" Abby asked. For a split second, Henry thought that might be amazing fun. It would be like they shared a superpower, but then he realized that he could still see his sister.

"I can see you. Can you see me?" he asked.

"Yeah," Abby said. "Maybe we canceled each other out."

Then Boo barked. They looked down at him. His tail was wagging, but his body was starting to fade. The white fur was almost invisible. The puppy's black dots lingered in the air for a moment more before he dashed off.

"It's Boo!" Henry yelled. "He's turned invisible!"

"Quick!" Abby yelled. "We have to get him!"

☆ Chapter 9 ☆

Henry and Abby paused just long enough to hear Boo's collar jingle as he ran down the stairs. Without a word, they were off. "You go to the kitchen and I'll go to the family room," Abby suggested. Henry did what his sister said. He ran into the kitchen, relieved that his dad wasn't there. Henry got down on his hands and knees to check all around Boo's bowl.

"Boo," he whispered. "Here, boy."

If the puppy had been in the kitchen, he would have come. He would have climbed in his lap and licked his face, but there was no Boo there. Henry got up and ran to find his sister. She wasn't in the family room anymore, so he decided to check the front hall. That's when he saw her. She was standing by the open front door.

His eyes locked with Abby's, and they shared the same fear. At that moment, their dad came bustling through the door, his shoulders weighed down with groceries. "Mom's home," he announced. "I tell you, Boo's dog food weighs a ton."

Henry and Abby took off out the door,

dodging their mom, who carried groceries in one hand and her briefcase in the other. "Good to see you playing together!" she called out as her kids raced by.

Henry and Abby stopped at the side of the house. "What are we going to do?" Abby said.

"Let's call him," Henry suggested. "He always comes."

"But Mom and Dad," Abby said. Henry knew what she meant. They might find out about the argument. They might find out that Boo got loose. They might find out about the trick.

"It doesn't matter. We have to find him," Henry said. "Maybe we should split up."

Abby shook her head. "I think we should do it together."

They started to call, taking turns. Henry saw his sister glance out toward the road. There was no way of knowing how far Boo might have gone. "Boo!" he yelled.

"Come here, boy!" Abby yelled. "What if he ran away?" Abby asked, stuffing her hands in her pockets. "He was pretty upset."

Henry remembered what Mr. Power had said that day at Power's Pets. If only he had thought about it before. They had not been careful when they asked Boo to do the trick.

They walked all around their yard, calling. They paused every few moments to see if they could hear the puppy's collar jangle.

"Why isn't he coming?" Henry was worried.

"Maybe he ran down the street," Abby said, dread in her voice. They started to backtrack, quickly passing the garage toward the front of the house.

Their dad was still unloading the car. "Hey, guys," he said. "What are you doing out here?"

Henry wasn't sure what to say, but Abby

didn't hesitate. "Dad, we lost Boo. We think he might have gotten out."

"Oh, no," Mr. McCoy answered. "Did you see where he went?"

"No," Abby admitted. "He ran past us and down the stairs."

"That's not good," their dad said. "We need to search."

"Wait, I hear scratching," Henry said. "It sounds like he's in the garage!"

"But I was just in there and didn't see him," Mr. McCoy said.

"It's him!" Abby yelped. She and Henry ran toward the front door.

"Boo!" they yelled, racing through the house.

Abby pushed herself against the door as she turned the knob, and they both burst into the garage.

"There, in the corner." Henry pointed. He could see faint black spots starting to reappear.

They rushed over. Abby reached out, with questioning hands, trying to feel the pup.

All at once, she threw back her head and started laughing. "He's licking me," she announced joyously. As Henry watched, Boo's pink tongue came into view. Henry immediately sat down next to his sister. He soon felt a pair of paws on his knees and saw an odd, floating tongue come at his chin. As Boo attacked Henry with happy slurps, his white fur started to fill in.

"Is he here?" Mr. McCoy asked from the doorway, turning on the light.

"Yes," Abby answered. Henry held his breath. What if his dad came all the way in? Boo wasn't invisible anymore, but he wasn't back to normal either. He looked like a ghost.

"He likes the ants," Abby said, offering a reason why the puppy had snuck into the garage.

"Well, he's the only one. It's so weird that I didn't see him in here before," their dad said, turning away. "I'm glad you found him."

Abby glanced over at Henry, and they shared a smile.

"That was close," Henry said.

"Too close," his sister agreed. "I think it's time to call a truce."

Henry nodded. "For Boo," he said.

"For Boo," Abby repeated.

Henry remembered the moment they picked out Boo at Power's Pets. It had seemed incredible that all the McCoys had wanted the same puppy. It was almost magical, how quickly the puppy had become a member of the family. Maybe his parents were right. Maybe sharing a puppy could help Henry and Abby figure out how to get along.

The brother-and-sister truce was an official agreement. Henry and Abby promised that they would never ask Boo to do his trick again. "We don't know what will happen," Henry had said.

"And we can't risk Boo turning invisible again," Abby added. "We could lose him forever."

At first, Henry was disappointed. Being invisible had been amazing. He hadn't even thought of all the cool stuff he could do. But Boo was more important. Both Abby and Henry agreed about that. Henry knew it was one promise they would both keep.

At dinner that night, Mr. McCoy was happy to announce that he had plugged up the hole where the ants came into the garage. "Boo was such a big help," he said. "If he hadn't been scratching in that corner, I never would have found the hole."

Hearing his name, Boo trotted over to the table. Mr. McCoy reached down and gave the puppy a loving pat on the back.

Mrs. McCoy wasn't sure that there was a solution to the ant problem. "Those pesky ants don't give up. They'll probably find another way in," she said. "Some things never change."

Yet some things did change. Abby and Henry had an announcement, too. "The science fair is next week. Since both of our projects were ruined, we decided to work on something new — together," Abby explained. "Henry and I are going to be partners."

"Well, that's good news," Mrs. McCoy said.

"And unexpected," Mr. McCoy added. "What's the new project?"

Henry drew in a big breath. It had felt surprisingly good to hear Abby call him her partner. He wondered if one day they might even be friends. Henry quickly brought himself back to reality and answered his dad's question. "We're going to do an experiment with Boo," he said. "We are going to see if he has a favorite color."

"Does he like to drink out of a blue or a red bowl better?" Abby said. Now Boo jogged around the table to where Abby was sitting. Abby gave him a long pet.

"Will he choose the red or the blue

squeeze toy?" Henry offered. Boo quickly moved over to Henry and nudged his leg. Henry reached down and scratched the puppy behind the ears. Boo snuffled his hand and gave him a sloppy lick.

"I think he'll go for blue," Abby said.

"No way," insisted Henry. "He likes red."

"Maybe he likes both," their mom suggested.

"He might," said Henry. He looked over at Abby. They shared an amazing puppy, and they would always agree on that. Henry gave his sister a sly smile. "But I think our science fair experiment will prove that he likes red best."

Puppy Powers

Read about the first puppy adopted at
Power's Pets in this special sneak peek!

Lexi crossed the street. When she got to Power's Pets, she gasped. The old toy store looked totally different. Yesterday, it had been empty. Today, it was full of animals and people.

As Lexi stepped inside, she saw a row of large cages lining one wall. They housed deluxe jungle gyms for hamsters, gerbils, and other tiny critters. Above Lexi's head, a jungle-green parrot perched on a swinging bar. There was a gigantic tank at the back of the store with bold red and electric-blue fish. The fish did loops and swirls together in perfect time. Three tabby kittens romped in a play area near the front window. The store felt festive, alive with happy chirps, squeaks, and chatter.

Lexi felt something cold and wet on her hand. She pulled her gaze from the kittens and looked down. There, at her feet, was the dog from the day before. He had something in his mouth. It was an envelope with her name written on it in green ink.

The dog sat down and looked up at Lexi with big brown eyes. His tail whipped back and forth in glee.

"He's excited to see you."

Lexi looked up. Mr. Power was walking toward her. He smiled. "Chance, I think you have something to give this young lady," he said. "Are you Lexi?" he asked, reading the name off her school envelope.

"Yes, I am," she said.

Chance whined and opened his mouth. Lexi took the envelope. "Thank you, Chance," she said, patting his head. "Where's your friend?"

"Oh, Lucky's watching the fish," Mr. Power explained. Lexi spotted the black cat sitting on top of the fish tank, staring down.

"Don't worry. Gus will make sure she keeps her paws to herself," the store's owner said with a smile.

Lexi looked more closely, and she saw a long-whiskered gray mouse plopped down next to the cat. She recognized him as the little mouse that had been in Mr. Power's pocket the day before.

"Welcome back to the store," Mr. Power said. "Would you like to meet a puppy?"

Mr. Power walked toward a large pen with a wooden gate. It was filled with shredded newspaper. Lexi saw lots of toys, but she didn't see a puppy.

Just then, a shiny black nose poked out from a pile of pillows. A fluffy puppy crawled out from under a red cushion. The puppy was mostly black with golden-brown markings above her eyes, across her chest, and on her legs. She gave herself a good shake, so her fuzzy fur puffed out even more.

"She's so cute!" Lexi said. It was true. She was the cutest puppy Lexi had ever seen.

Rrruff, ruff, the puppy barked. She trotted toward Lexi and put her front legs up on the side of the pen. *Rrruff, ruff!*

Lexi looked up at Mr. Power.

"I think she wants you to pick her up," he said.

Lexi quickly bent down and swooped the puppy into her arms. She was so soft! "Hey, you," Lexi whispered, and the puppy responded with a sloppy lick of Lexi's nose. Lexi giggled. As she pulled away, she noticed a shiny brass tag hanging from the puppy's collar. It read LUNA.

WHERE EVERY PUPPY FINDS A HOME

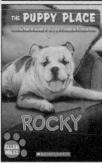
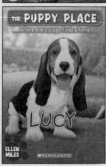

SCHOLASTIC
www.scholastic.com
www.ellenmiles.net

Read them all!